David A. Johnson

Snow
Sounds

An Onomatopoeic Story

Houghton Mifflin Company ✷ 2006

hush

Swoosh
Slush
Smoosh

Swoosh slush slush smoosh

Crash
Crush
Clank

Crash Crush **Clank**

beep

beep

beep

beep

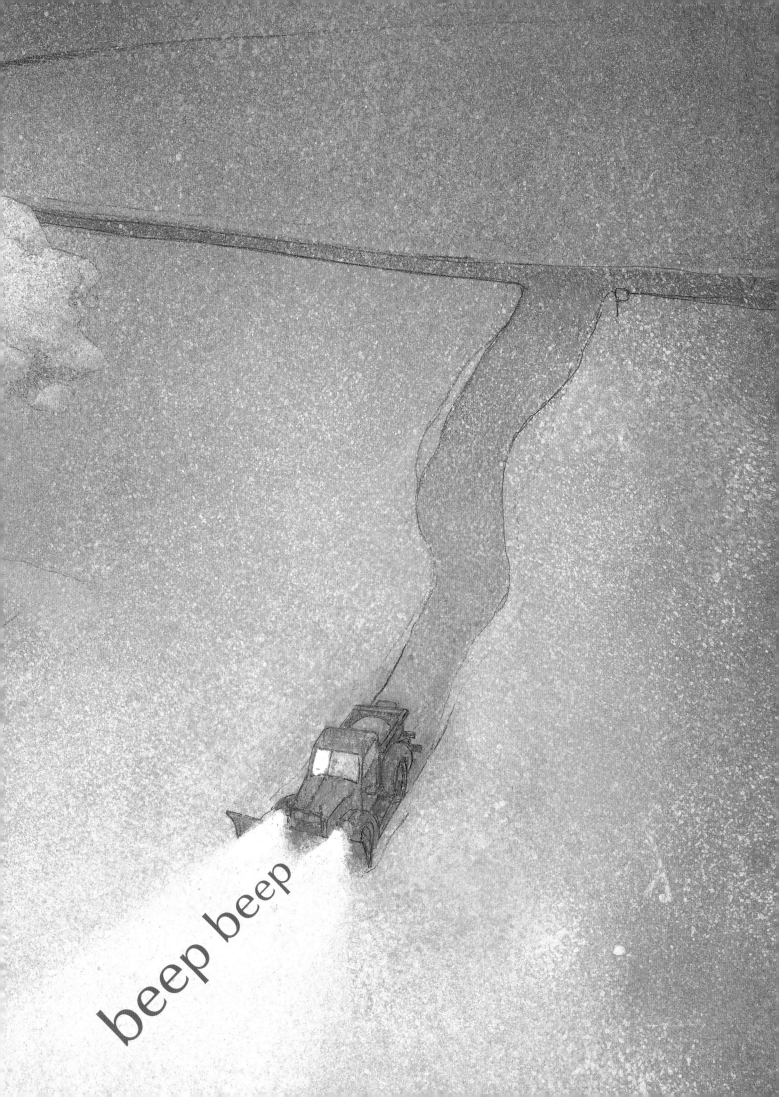

chug

chug

whoosh

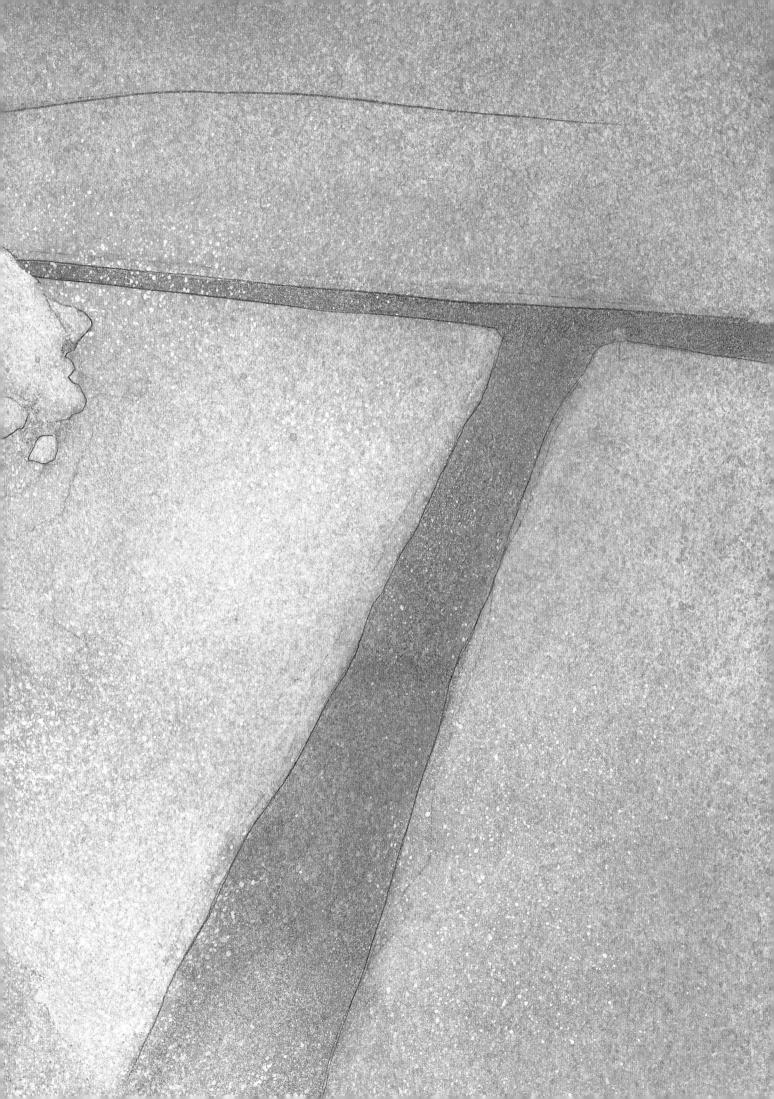

Bump

Shuffle Shuffle

Jingle Clink Clinky Jingly

Scoop
Scrape

HONK HONK

Whomp

"Wait!"

I couldn't have done it myself.
Frank and I made the snow go away,
Ann and I made the book appear.
Thank you.
— D. A. J.

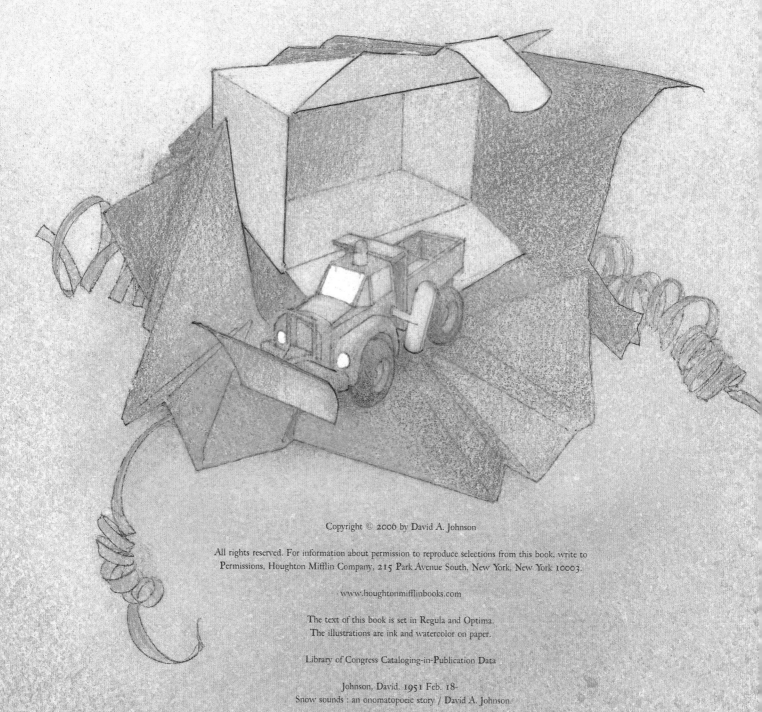

All rights reserved. For information about permission to reproduce selections from this book, write to
Permissions, Houghton Mifflin Company, 215 Park Avenue South, New York, New York 10003.

www.houghtonmifflinbooks.com

The text of this book is set in Regula and Optima.
The illustrations are ink and watercolor on paper.

Library of Congress Cataloging-in-Publication Data

Johnson, David, 1951 Feb. 18-
Snow sounds : an onomatopoeic story / David A. Johnson.
p. cm.
Summary: A nearly wordless book in which a young boy, eager to reach a much-anticipated holiday
party on time, listens to the sounds of the shovels, snowplow, and other equipment used to clear his way.
ISBN-13: 978-0-618-47310-6 (hardcover)
ISBN-10: 0-618-47310-6 (hardcover)
[1. Snow removal—Fiction. 2. Sounds, Words for.] I. Title.
PZ7.J6 1631 1 5Sno 2006
[E]—dc22

2006000333

Manufactured in China
SCP 10 9 8 7 6 5 4 3 2 1